FRAZZLE

Written by Stephen Cosgrove
Illustrated by Robin James

A Serendipity™ Book

PSS!
PRICE STERN SLOAN

Dedicated to the March of Dimes
and the years and years of marches that
helped those things that hurt us.

— Stephen

Beyond the horizon, farther than far, in the middle of the Crystal Sea, was a beautiful island called Serendipity. On the island was a tree, a great and wondrous tree, where winged life wheeled and reeled on the winds that gently blew in and about its boughs and branches.

This tree was called the Dream Tree, the beginning of all feathered life on the island of Serendipity.

It was in and around this tree of dreams that all the birds of Serendipity came to lay their eggs, the beginning of new winged life to come. The Dream Tree was filled with the sounds of their joyful twittering.

Mothers-to-be of every feathered form—eagle, gull, and all others—came here to the spreading arms of this great tree to take shelter during this wondrous time of life. They would carefully fly into the tree where they would wait until it was time to lay their egg or eggs, as the case might be.

Now, it seems that not all the birds that came here knew quite what was going on. One of these slightly confused mothers was a fat little ruffle-feather called Frazzle.

One day it seemed she was but a fledgling chick herself and the next day she was a mother-to-be. Now she sat on a broad branch, and in the mottled light of the shaded tree she watched all the goings-on in wonder.

She watched as the other mother birds carefully exercised while they waited for their eggs to be laid and then to hatch. Frazzle didn't join in for she didn't believe in exercise. She felt that sitting was exercise enough, especially if you were watching others exercise.

She watched as the other birds ate bugs and worms and berries, which were all healthy foods for birds indeed. Unfortunately, Frazzle was not very fond of such things. She thought bugs tasted like bugs and worms tasted like dirt. So, instead of bird-healthy food, she ate sugared wonders that she found in the castle nearby. She got downright fat, and the branch nearly snapped from her weight.

As was the custom, the other birds carefully fashioned nests from velvet leaves and bits of soft grasses they collected all over the meadow. Their nursery nests had been woven in the softest and most delicate fashion, for it was here that the eggs would hatch and the new baby birds would be born. The other mother birds would sit in their nests nurturing and warming the eggs that they had laid sometime before.

This day, however, the tree was atwitter as Frazzle built the shabbiest nest from bits of paper, sticks, and mud. Everyone watched in shock as she threw this together with that to build a nest that was neither neat nor nice. When she was done, she flopped into the mess she had made and ate a candy cane left over from the Season of Snow.

One day, as nature would have it, Frazzle felt an odd sensation, a twitching in her tummy. She flopped back to her nest, which was neither neat nor nice, and sat down with a thump. With a grunt and a groan, and not just a little bit of pain, she laid one very large egg.

"Wow!" said Frazzle, relieved. "Bird howdy, am I ever glad that's over with." And with that she spread her wings to fly away.

"Where are you going?" the other birds asked, as she began flapping her wings.

"Why, I'm going for a fly," laughed Frazzle, "and then I thought I would plop down in that patch of honeysuckle down by the creek and sip some sugared dew that flows through the vine. Do you want to come?"

"Harumph," muttered one of the birds indignantly. "We can't go, and neither can you."

"What? Why?" asked Frazzle, all frazzled, her feathers fluttered.

"Because," croaked an old mother crow, "laying the egg is just the beginning. Now you must sit softly upon the egg and keep it warm until it hatches."

"Well," grumbled Frazzle, "I guess I can stick around a few more days."

So Frazzle perched near the nest and occasionally sat on the egg. But, for the most part, she would disappear from time to time looking for goodies to eat.

When daylight turned to dusk turned to dark, all the other birds fell fast asleep, for a good night's sleep is important for a healthy mother. Not Frazzle. She would hop to the outside edge of the tree, and for hours and hours she would chirp with night owls that prowled the night skies.

Though the others warned her that she needed her sleep, Frazzle didn't listen at all.

It wasn't bad enough that Frazzle didn't eat foods that were good for her. It wasn't bad enough that she never exercised and was getting full in the feather, fat, if you would. It wasn't bad enough that she never got enough sleep.

But what was bad enough, if bad can even be worse or worst, was that Frazzle was ignoring her egg.

That beautiful egg, all bright light blue and covered in glitz and glimmer, had begun to fade. The egg started looking just as bad, if not worse, than Frazzle herself.

Frazzle knew that she had to sit on the egg and keep it warm, but she had eaten so much that every time she scrunched herself down in the nest, the egg groaned in protest. The egg rolled this way and that way trying to get out of her way as she sat with a thump—her big rump just one big clump of feathers and fluff.

That poor egg didn't know what was worse: being cold or being crushed.

One day as Frazzle sat on her mess of a nest she began to study the other mothers in the tree. Their beaks seemed to glow and their feathers were fluffy and fine. Their eggs, healthy blue in color, nestled in clean, downy nests.

She looked and she looked, and the more she looked the more she knew that she had done something very, very wrong. A solitary, sugary tear seeped like syrup from the corner of Frazzle's eye and plopped like a gumdrop into the nest.

Now the other birds, who for all practical purposes had ignored Frazzle as much as she had ignored them, became silent and still as Frazzle's one tear turned into a torrent and she began to sob out loud, "Oh, what have I done to my baby!"

"There, there, dear," the other mothers chirped, "what can the matter be?"

"What can the matter be?" cried Frazzle. "I am fat and you are thin. My egg is faded and yours are bright blue. Everything is the matter, and there is nothing, nothing that I can do."

"Ah," they laughed as they fluttered to her side, "there is everything you can do. You can eat better, not more. You can walk, not sit. For you are what your baby will be."

Frazzle looked down into her reflection cast from the puddle of her tears. What she saw wasn't pretty, and if her baby were to be like her, it was a sad state of affairs indeed. "If I am what my baby will be, then my baby will be a sugar-coated hippopotamus."

"And," one of the birds chirped lightly, "it is never too late to right a wrong."

From that day forward all the other birds helped Frazzle turn her wrongs to rights. She learned all the right things to do for her body. She ate good foods, not sugared, and she exercised as much as she could. She never became slender, her feathers never turned to gold, but inside, she became an eagle — proud of herself and bold.

Oh and yes, the egg gained back its luster and once again became bright, light-blue, covered with spots of glitz and glimmer. Frazzle now knew that her egg could be anything that she could be and maybe even a little bit better.

ONE DAY IT FINALLY HAPPENED
IN THE BLINK AND WINK OF AN EYE,
FRAZZLE'S EGG CRACKED WIDE OPEN—
"HUSH, HUSH, SWEET BABY DON'T CRY"

Serendipity™ Books

Created by
Stephen Cosgrove and Robin James

Enjoy all the delightful books in the Serendipity™ Series:

Available wherever books are sold.

PSS!
PRICE STERN SLOAN